How well do you *really* know your dog?

Have you ever wondered where dogs go and what they do while you're asleep at night? Well, the little boy in this story has reason to believe that his dog has something funny going on, and he's ready to find out what it is. Join him on his hilarious adventure.

Praise for *The Night I Followed the Dog*

"Sophisticated enough for older children and silly enough for younger listeners, this boy-and-his-dog book has clever text, great illustrations, and strong appeal."
—*School Library Journal*

"Stylish, droll. . . . A salutary outing."
—*Publishers Weekly*

"Whimsical." —*Kirkus Reviews*

"[A] comedic gem. . . . This zany debut is cause for celebration."
—Parents' Choice Foundation

"Wonderful. . . . A typographic delight." —*Newsday*

A Parents' Choice Gold Award winner
A Children's Choice Book Award winner
A Bookbuilders West Design Award winner

In memory of my mother,
who would have been so proud.

For Booth.

Special thanks to Victoria Rock, Kendra Marcus,
and to Beth for being on a ferry on Lake Como.

First Chronicle Books LLC paperback edition, published in 2017.
Originally published in hardcover in 1994 by Chronicle Books LLC.

ISBN 978-1-4521-6134-1

The Library of Congress has cataloged the original edition as follows:
Laden, Nina.
      The night I followed the dog / Nina Laden.
              p.   cm.
      Summary: A boy follows his dog one night to see exactly what dogs do at night when they're on their own.
ISBN-10: 0-8118-0647-2 ISBN-13: 978-0-8118-0647-3
      [1. Dogs—Fiction. 2. Imagination—Fiction. 3. Night—Fiction.]
I. Title.
PZ7.L13735Ni   1994
[E]—dc2093-31008
             CIP
             AC

Manufactured in China.

MIX
Paper from responsible sources
FSC® C008047

Book design by Cathleen O'Brien.
Text handwritten by Nina Laden. Flaps typeset in Futura.
The illustrations in this book were rendered in chalk pastels on Strathmore Artagain Gotham gray paper.

10 9 8 7 6 5 4 3 2 1

Chronicle Books LLC
680 Second Street
San Francisco, California 94107

Chronicle Books—we see things differently. Become part of our community at www.chroniclekids.com.

The Night I Followed The Dog

WORDS AND PICTURES BY NINA LADEN

Chronicle Books San Francisco

I have a dog. Nothing exotic or special, just an ordinary dog. In fact, I always thought he was a boring dog. What I mean is, he can Fetch, ROLL OVER, and shake hands, but mostly he sleeps and EATS.

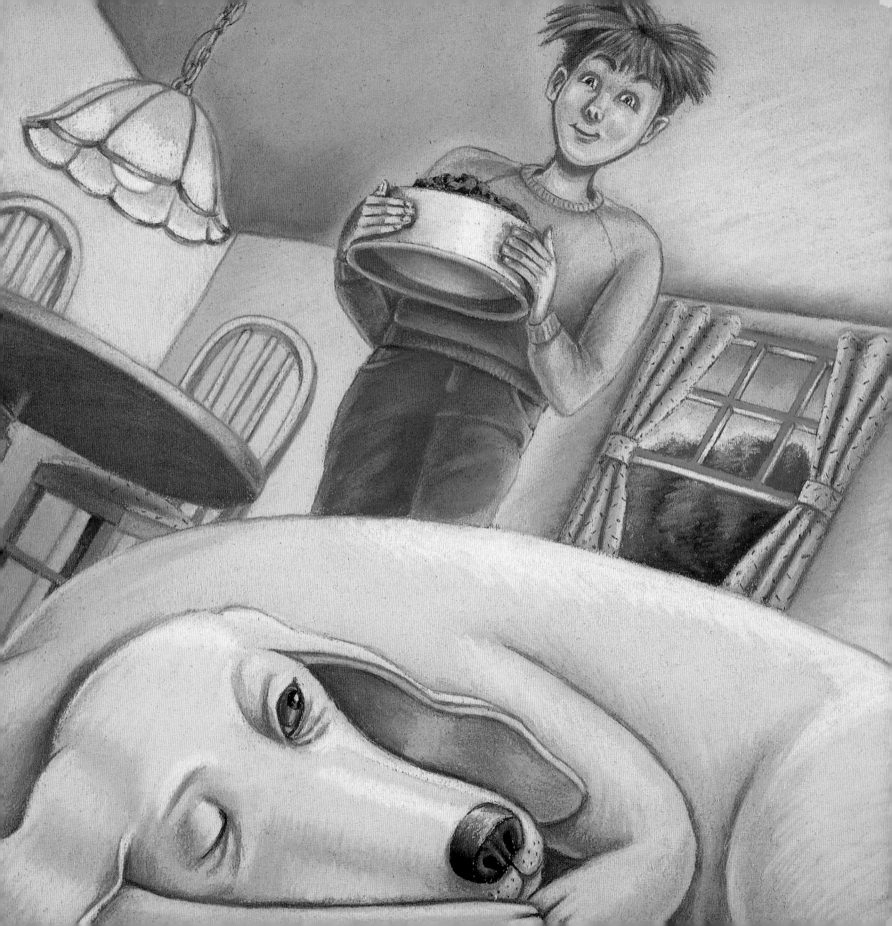

I used to think that our next-door neighbors had the best dog in the world. Their dog can sing and change the channels on the TV. Their dog always wins MEDALS in obedience school. But I don't think their dog is so great now — not since the night I followed **MY** dog.

Every night, I let my dog out, and he runs off into the darkness with his tail **wagging**. The next morning I let him in, and he heads straight for the food bowl. But one morning I knew something was **FUNNY** when I opened the door a little bit earlier than usual, and I saw my dog jump out of a **LIMOUSINE** . . .

wearing a tuxedo.

Before I could look twice, he **DISAPPEARED** into the backyard. I opened the kitchen door and *whistled.* When he came into the house he was the same as he always is, **hungry.** I really wasn't sure that I believed what I had seen, so that night I decided to follow him.

I wore DARK CLOTHING, so I wouldn't be noticed, and I left my bicycle near the door, so I'd have it close by. When I let the dog out, I slipped out, too. I took out the garbage, so he wouldn't suspect anything. The dog went straight to his doghouse. I saw a light go on inside. **SLOWLY**, I snuck around the backyard, and peeked into the doghouse.

This was not the doghouse that I had helped build. Inside, there was a living room, a bathroom, and a **HUGE** closet full of Fancy clothes. The dog was in the bathroom. He was wearing a tuxedo and **Fumbling** with the bow tie. When he came out, he casually walked out of the doghouse, across the yard, and down the street.

I grabbed my bicycle and followed him. Two blocks later, I saw a LIMOUSINE pull over. The dog got in, and the car took off. I started pedaling **FASTER**. The car headed across town. I thought I would lose them, but luckily they were stopped by a few red lights.

After a while, I found myself in a part of town that I had never seen before. The buildings all seemed to be empty, and it was very quiet. The limousine stopped. I hid and watched my dog get out. He DISAPPEARED into a building, and the limousine pulled away.

There was nothing on the outside of the building, just two BRASS fire hydrants on either side of the entrance. I opened the door. At the end of the hall there was a NEON sign that said "The Doghouse." I crept closer. It looked like some kind of club. I decided to get a CLOSER look.

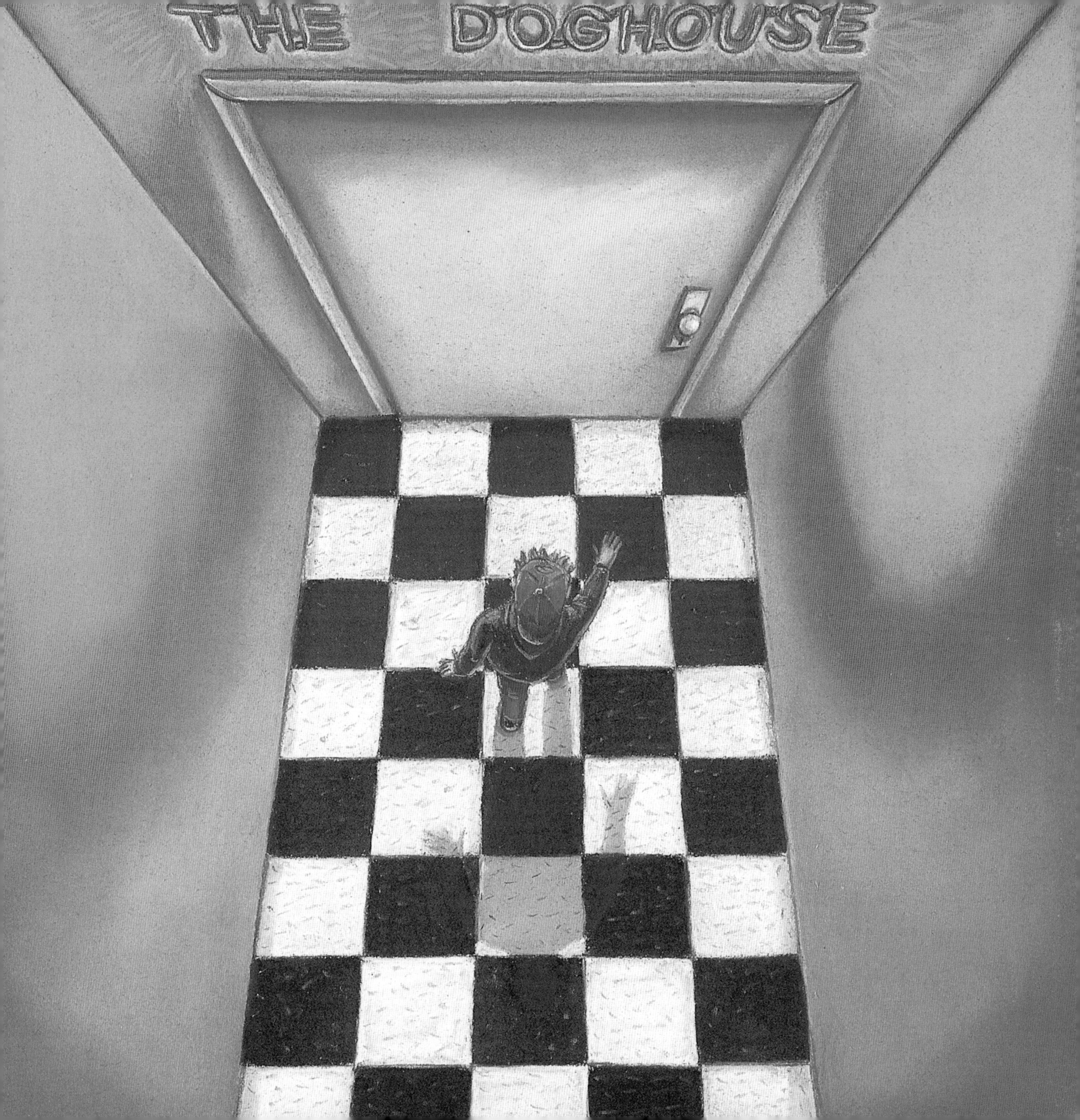
THE DOGHOUSE

The moment I opened the door two **MEAN** looking bulldogs appeared and said, "You can't come in here!" I didn't know what to say, so I said, "B-but, b-but I saw my dog ... I mean, I think my dog's in here." Just then, my dog walked over and said, "It's okay, boys, he's with me." The bulldogs said, "Sure, **Boss**. Whatever you say, **Boss**."

For a minute that seemed like forever, I waited. Then my dog said, "I knew you would find out eventually. Well, now you know. This is my place." I looked around. Finally, I asked, "What is this place?" My dog said, "This? This is a place where dogs come after a hard day. It's a place where we can **relax**. It's a place where we can talk about our problems with the MAILMAN, or with the **poodle** next door."

"See all the sofas? We can **sit** on the sofas here. We can get treats without having to SHAKE HANDS, ROLL OVER, or play dead. And if we want to chew on a shoe or CHASE OUR TAIL, no one will stop us. We have no masters here, no *leashes*, and no rolled up newspapers. This? This is a place where dogs can be dogs."

We sat down. A cocker spaniel came by and asked me if I would like a bowl of water, or some BISCUITS. Little by little, dogs of all kiNDS started coming in. Some danced, some TALKED. They all looked at me a little funny, but when they saw who I was with, they smiled, and shook my hand.

At one point, my dog waved to an afghan with a camera. She came over to our table and took a Picture of us together. Being with my dog made me feel like a movie star.

Just when I was really starting to enjoy myself, I looked at my watch. I told my dog I had to leave, or I'd get in **TROUBLE**. He nodded. I think he was about to say something, but a **Glamorous** greyhound grabbed his paw and whisked him onto the dance floor. As he was getting up, he tossed me the **PHOTO** of the two of us. Then he bowed slightly and disappeared into the **CROWD**.

It was way past my bedtime. As I pedaled home into the COOL night, I thought to myself, "Now I'm really going to be in the doghouse." But then again, that might not be so bad.

THE END

Nina Laden is the author and illustrator of many books for children, including *Peek-a Who?*, one of Scholastic *Parent & Child* Magazine's 100 Greatest Books for Kids; its companions *Peek-a Zoo!*, *Peek-a Boo!*, and *Peek-a Choo-Choo!*; *Roberto: The Insect Architect*; *When Pigasso Met Mootisse*; *Are We There Yet?*; and *Once Upon a Memory*, illustrated by Renata Liwska. She lives in Seattle and Lummi Island, Washington.